# WREN

For Nic, Charlotte, Sunday and Finn,
who never cease to surprise me and inspire me.
And for Mum and Dad, who gave me a childhood that dreams are made of.
—Katrina

To my mum Jacqueline.
Through the noise and chaos, your love was always there.
—Sophie

# WREN

WRITTEN BY
## KATRINA LEHMAN

ILLUSTRATED BY
## SOPHIE BEER

SCRIBBLE

The illustrations in this book are made with a combination of traditional mark making and digital medium.

Typeset in Bodoni Egyptian by the Publisher.

Published by Scribble, an imprint of Scribe Publications, 2018
This edition published in 2021
18–20 Edward Street, Brunswick, Victoria 3056, Australia
2 John Street, Clerkenwell, London, WC1N 2ES, United Kingdom
3754 Pleasant Ave, Suite 100, Minneapolis, Minnesota 55409 USA
This book is printed on FSC® paper. Printed and bound in China by Leo Paper Products Ltd
9781925322118 (Australian hardback)
9781911617266 (UK paperback)
9781925849172 (Australian paperback)
9781950354665 (North American hardback)
CiP records for this title are available from the National Library of Australia
scribblekidsbooks.com
scribepublications.com.au

Wren didn't like noise.

Trucks rumbling and bumbling.
Bikes wheeling and squealing.

Cars hooting. Trains tooting.
Kids stamping and stomping
and screeching.

Doors slamming. Dogs barking.
Kettles whistling. Dishes clanging.

The telephone ringing. The neighbor singing.
And parents talking — on and on and on.

All Wren wanted was
a little bit of peace and quiet.

WREN'S
HOUSE

But what he got was a baby sister.

Wren had never heard anything like her!

WAHHHHWAHHHHWAHHHHWAHHHHWAHHHHWAH

She yelled when she was hungry.
She cried when she was tired.
She screeched when she was upset.

She was louder than a train
and wailed for longer
than a fire engine.

His mother talked to her and walked with her.

His brothers played music for her,
and his sister sang to her.

But she just screamed
until the house shook.
All day long
and all night long.

Wren tried closing his bedroom door and blocking it out.

He tried sleeping in the garden.

Eventually, he decided the only thing to do was move in with Grandpa and Gram.

Permanently.

The country was quiet.

No noisy neighbors.

No traffic.

No sisters and brothers.

Just fields and trees and the big blue sky.

But after a week, Wren started to feel strange.

He missed trucks rumbling and bumbling
and bikes wheeling and squealing.
He missed doors slamming. Dogs barking. Kettles whistling.

He even missed his sisters and brothers
stamping and stomping and screeching.

And he couldn't help wondering:
Did his baby sister like her new family?

Perhaps it was time to go home.

When Wren arrived home, nothing had changed.

'Oh Wren, it's lovely to have you back,'
said his mother.
'You know, I think the baby missed you.
Would you like to give her a cuddle?'

Wren slowly reached out
for his wailing sister.

He had never held her before.
She was so warm. So small.

He sat down and began to rock.
He didn't talk. He didn't sing.
He just rocked.

His little sister stopped crying.
Surprised blue eyes looked into his.

She curled a tiny fist around
his finger and opened her
mouth again...

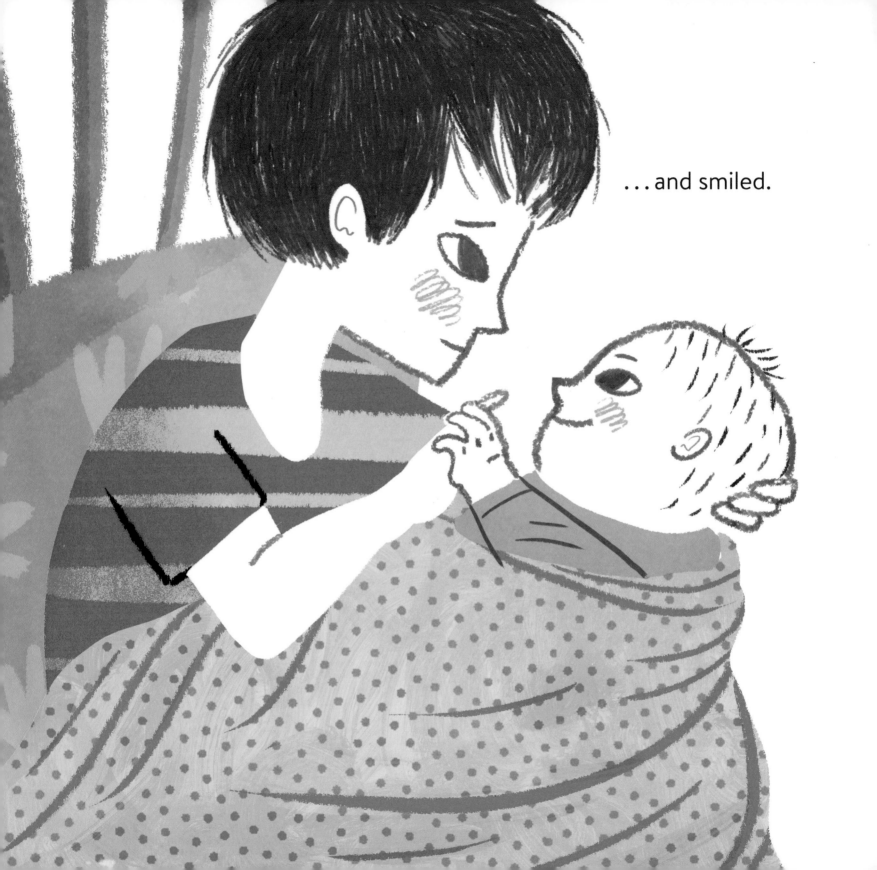

. . . and smiled.

Then she closed her eyes and went to sleep. Wren sat for a long time and stared at his baby sister. And then he smiled too.

Perhaps all she wanted was a little bit of peace and quiet.

Just like him.

METEORS

BEAR